THE DARK INTRUDER

THE DARK INTRUDER

by Marion Zimmer Bradley

ANDREW SLAYTON snapped the dusty *leather* notebook shut, and tossed it into his blanket roll. He stood up, ducking to avoid the ridgepole of the tent—Andrew, who had grown up on low-gravity Mars, was just over seven feet tall—and stood up, his head a little bent, looking at the other men who shared this miniature outpost against the greatest desert ever known to man.

The flaps of the tent were tightly pegged against the fierce and unpredictable sandstorms of the Martian night. In the glow of a portable electric lamp, the four roughnecks who would do the actual digging squatted around an up-ended packing box, intent on tonight's installment of their perpetual poker game.

A dark oblong in the corner of the tent rose and fell with regular snores. John Reade, temporary leader of this expedition, was not young, and the day's work had been exhausting.

The men glanced up from their cards as Slayton approached them. "Want to sit in, kid?" Mike Fairbanks asked, "Kater's losing his shirt. We could use a new dealer."

"No, thanks. Not tonight."

Fat Kater shook with laughter, and jeered "The kid'ud rather read about Kingslander's men, and how they all went nuts and shot each other up!"

Spade Hansen flung down his cards, with a gesture of annoyance. "That's nothing to joke about, Kater." He lowered his gruff voice. "Find anything in the logs, Andy?"

Andrew squatted, elbows on thighs, beside the big foreman. "Nothing but what we know already, Spade. It beats me. As near as I can figure out, Jack Norton's expedition—he only had ten men—was washed up inside a week. Their rations are still cached over there. And, according to Kingslander's notebook, his outfit went the same way. They reached here safely, made camp, did a little exploring—they found the bodies of Norton's men and buried them—then, one by one, they all went insane and shot each other. Twenty men—and within ten days, they were just twenty-corpses."

"Pleasant prospect," Kater glowered, slapping down his cards on the improvised table and scowling as Rick Webber raked in the pot. "What about us?"

Rick Webber meticulously stacked his winnings and scaled his cards at Hensen. "Quit your worrying. Third time lucky— maybe we'll get through, all right."

"And maybe we won't," Fairbanks grunted, raking the cards together and shuffling them with huge fists, "You know what they call this outfit back in Mount Denver? *Reade's Folly.*"

"I'd hate to tell you what they called the first men who actually tried *living* on Mars," said a sleepy, pleasant voice from the corner, and John Reade thrust up his shock of white hair. "But we're here." The old man turned to Andrew. "Wasn't there even a clue in the logs, some notion of what might have happened to them?"

Andrew swivelled to face him. "Not a word, sir. Kings-lander kept the log himself until he was shot, then one of his men—Ford Benton—kept it. The last couple of pages are the most awful gibberish—not even in English. Look for yourself—he was obviously but of his head for days." Andrew unfolded his long legs, hauled up a corner of the tent flap, and stood, staring morosely across the dark wasteland of rocks and bare bushes, toward the looming mass of Xanadu.

Xanadu. Not the Xanadu of Coleridge's poem, but—to the half-forgotten space drifter who discovered the place thirty years ago—a reasonable facsimile. It was a cloistered nun of a city, hidden behind a wide skirt of the most impassable mountains on Mars. And the city was more impassable than the mountains. No human being had ever entered it—yet.

They'd tried. Two expeditions, twelve years apart, had vanished without trace, without explanation other than the dusty notebook Andrew had unearthed, today, from the rotted shreds of a skeleton's clothing.

Archaeological expeditions., on Mars, all start the same way. You argue, wheedle, beg, borrow and steal until you have the necessary authority and a little less than the necessary funds. Earth, torn with internecine wars and slammed down under currency restrictions, does not send much money to Mars at any time. All but the barest lifeline of supplies was choked off when it was finally verified that Mars had no heavy metals, very little worth mining. The chronically-bankrupt Geographical Society had abandoned Mars even before Xanadu was discovered. The thronging ruins of Venus, the strange surviving culture of subterranean men on Titan, the odd temples of the inner moons of Jupiter, are more rewarding than the desert barrens of Mars and its inaccessible Xanadu—the solitary remnant of a Martian society which must have vanished before mankind, on Earth, had discovered fire.

For all practical purposes, Mars is a military frontier, patrolled by the U.N. to keep any one country from using it as a base for developing secret weapons. It's also a good place to test new atomic engines, since there isn't much of a fallout problem and no worry about a large population getting fallout jitters. John Reade, retired Major in the Space Service, had good military contacts, and had managed to get a clearance for the third—only the third—attempt to conquer Xanadu.

Private expeditions on Mars are simple to the point of being primitive. No private citizen or foundation could possibly pay freight charges for machinery to Mars. Private citizens travel on foot, taking with them only what they can carry on their backs. Besides, no one could take a car, a plane or a rocketship over the mountains and still find a safe place to land. Pack animals are out of the question; horses and burros cannot adapt to the thin air—thicker than pre-space theorists had dared to hope, but still pretty thin—and dogs and chimpanzees, which can, aren't—much good for pack-work. The Geographic Society is still debating about importing yaks and llamas from high-altitude Peru and Tibet; meanwhile, it's a good thing that gravity on Mars is low enough to permit tremendous packloads of necessities.

The prime necessity is good lungs and a sackful of guts, while you scramble, scratch and curse your way over the mountains. Then a long, open valley, treacherously lined with needles of rock, and Xanadu lying—the bait in the mouth of the trap—at the top.

And then—what?

Kater and Hansen and the rest were grumbling over the cards again. "This place is jinxed," Mike complained, turning up a deuce. "We'll be lucky if we get a cent out of it Now if we were working on Venus—but Mars, nyaah! Even if we find something, which I doubt, and live to tell about it—who cares?"

"Yeah," Spade muttered. "Reade, how much did you spend for dynamite to blast the walls?"

"You didn't pay for it," Reade said cheerfully.

Andrew stooped, shrugging on his leather jacket; thumbed the inside heating-units. "I'm going for a walk."

"Alone?" Reade asked sharply.

"Sure, unless someone wants to come along," Andrew said, then suddenly understood. He pulled his pistol from his pocket, and handed it, butt-first, to Reade. "Sorry, I should have remembered. This is about where the shooting started, with the others."

Reade laughed, but he didn't return the gun.

"Don't go too far."

It was one of the rare, clear nights which sometimes did penance for the usual sandstorms. Andrew drew down the tent flap behind him, walked away into the darkness. At his foot he felt a little scurrying, stooped and caught up one of the blunt-nosed sand-mice. It squirmed on his palm, kicking hard with all six puny legs; then felt the comforting heat of his hand and yeep-yeeped with pleasure; he walked on, idly scratching the scaly little beast.

The two small moons were high overhead, and there was a purplish, shimmery light over the valley, with its grotesque floor of rock spires, fuzzed between with blackish patches of prickle-bushes—*spinosa martts*—matted in a close tangle between each little peak.

Downwind he heard the long screaming of a banshee; then he saw it, running blindly, a huge bird with its head down between trailing, functionless wings. Andrew held his breath and stood still. The banshees had no intelligence to speak of, but by some peculiar tropism, they would rush toward anything that moved; the very heat of his body might attract them, and their huge clawed feet could disembowel a man at one stroke. And he had no pistol!

This one failed to sense him; it ran, trailing its wings and screaming eerily, like a cloaked girl, blindly into the dusk. Andrew let out his breath violently in relief. Suddenly he realized that he was not sure just which way the tent lay. He turned, crowding against "one of the rockspires. A little hollow gleamed pallidly in the moonlight. He remembered climbing a rise; he must have come this way—

He slid down roughly, a trailing pricker raking his hand. The sand-mouse leaped from his palm with a squeal and scuffled away. Andrew, sucking his bleeding palm, looked up and saw the walls of Xanadu lifting serried edges just over his head. How could he possibly have come so near in just a few minutes? Everything looked different—

He spun around, trying to scramble up the way he had come. He fell. His head struck rock, and the universe went dark.

"Take it easy." John Reade's voice sounded disembodied over his head,

"Just lie still. You've got a bad bump, Andy."

He opened his eyes to the glare of stars and a bitter wind on his face. Reade caught at his hand ~ as he moved it exploringly toward his face. "Let it alone, the bleeding's stopped. What happened? The banshee get you?"

"No, I fell. I lost my way, and I must have hit my head." Andrew let his eyes fall shut again. "I'm sorry, sir; I know you told us not to go near the city alone. But I didn't realize I'd come so close."

Reade frowned and leaned closer. "Lost your *way?* What are you talking about? I followed you—brought your pistol. I was afraid you'd meet a banshee. You hadn't gone two hundred yards from the tent, Andy. When I caught up with you, you were stumbling around, and then you rolled down on the ground into that little hollow. You kept muttering *No, no, no—*I thought the banshee had got you."

Andrew pushed himself upright. "I don't think so, sir. I looked up and saw the city right over my head. That's what made me fall. That's when it started."

"When *what* started?"

"I—don't know." Andrew put up his hand to rub his forehead, wincing as he touched the bruise. Suddenly he asked "John, did you ever wonder what the old Martians—the ones who built Xanadu—called the place?"

"Who hasn't?" The old man nodded, impatiently. "I guess we'll never know, though. That's a fool question to ask me right now!"

"It's something I felt," Andrew said, groping for words. "When I got up, after I stumbled, everything looked different. It was like seeing double; one part was just rocks, and bushes, and ruins, and the other part was—well, it wasn't like anything I'd ever seen before. I felt—" he hesitated, searching for words to define something strange, then said with an air of surprise, "*Homesick.* Yes, that's it. And the most awful—desolation. The way I'd feel, I guess, if I went back to Mount Denver and found it burned down flat. And then for just a second I knew what the city was called, and why it was dead, and why we couldn't get into it, and why tie other men went crazy. And it scared me, and I started to run—and that's when I slipped, and hit my head."

Reade's worried face relaxed in a grin.

"Rubbish! The bump on your head mixed up your timesense a little, that's all. Your hallucination, or whatever it was, came *after* the bump, not before."

"No," Andrew said quietly, but with absolute conviction. "I wasn't hurt that bad, John."

Reade's face changed; held concern again, "All right," he said gently, "Tell me what you think you know."

Andrew dropped his face in his hands. "Whatever it was, it's gone! The bump knocked it right out of my head. I remember that I knew—" he raised a drawn face, "but I can't remember what!"

Reade put his hand on the younger man's shoulder. "Let's get back to the tent, Andy, I'm freezing out here. Look, son, the whole thing is just your mind working overtime from that bump you got. Or—"

Andrew said bitterly, "You think I'm going crazy."

"I didn't say that, son. Come on. We can talk it over in the morning." He hoisted Andrew to his feet. "I told Spade that if we weren't back in half an hour, he'd better come looking for us."

The men looked up from their cards, staring at the blood on Andrew's face, but the set of Reade's mouth silenced any comments. Andrew didn't want to talk. He quickly shucked jacket and trousers, crawled into his sleeping bag, thumbed the heat-unit and immediately fell asleep.

When he woke, the tent was empty. Wondering why he had been allowed to sleep—Spade usually meted out rough treatment to blanket-huggers—Andrew dressed quickly, gulped a mug of the bitter coffee that stood on the hot-box, and went out to look for the others.

He had to walk some distance to find them. Armed with shovels, the four roughnecks were digging up the thorny prickle-bushes near the hollow where Andrew had fallen, while Reade, in the lee of a rock, was scowling over the fine print of an Army manual of Martio-biology.

"Sorry I overslept, John. Where do I go to work?"

"You don't. I've got another job for you." Reade turned to bark a command at Fairbanks. "Careful with the damned plant! I told you to wear gloves! Now get them on, and don't touch those things with your bare hands." He glanced back at Andrew. "I had an idea overnight," he said. "What do we really know about *spinosa martis*? And this doesn't quite look like the species that grows around Mount Denver. I think maybe this variety gives off some kind of gas—or poison." He pointed at the long scratch on Andrew's hand. "Your trouble started after you grabbed one of them. You know, there's locoweed on Earth that drives cattle crazy-

mushrooms and other plants that secrete hallucinogens. If these things give off some sort of volatile mist, it could have dispersed in that little hollow down there—there wasn't much wind last night."

"What shall I do?" he asked.

"I'd rather not discuss that here. Come on, I'll walk back to the tent with you." He scrambled stiffly to his feet. "I want you to go back to Mount Denver, Andy."

Andrew stopped; turned to Reade accusingly.

"You *do* think I've gone crazy!"

Reade shook his head. "I just think you'll be better off in Mount Denver. —I've got a job for you there—one man would have to go, anyhow, and you've had one—well, call it a hallucination—already. If it's a poison, the stuff might be cumulative. We may just wind up having to wear gas masks." He put a hand on the thick leather of Andrew's jacket sleeve. "I know how you feel about this place, Andy. But personal feelings aren't important in this kind of work."

"John—" half hesitant, Andrew looked back at him, "I had an idea overnight, too."

"Let's hear it."

"It sounds crazy, I guess," Andrew said diffidently, "but it just came to me. Suppose the old Martians were beings without bodies—discarnate intelligences? And they're trying to make contact with us? Men aren't used to that kind of contact, and it drives them insane."

Reade scowled. "Ingenious," he admitted,, "as a theory, but there's a hole in it. If they're discarnate, how did they build—" he jerked his thumb at the squat, fortress-like mass of Xanadu behind them.

"I don't know, sir. I don't know how the drive units of a spaceship work, either. But I'm here." He looked up. "I think one of them was trying to get in touch with me, last night. And maybe if I was trying, too—maybe if I understood, and tried to open my mind to it, too—"

Reade looked disturbed. "Andy, do you realize what you're suggesting? Suppose this is all your imagination—"

"It isn't, John."

"Wait, now. Just suppose, for a minute; try to see it my way."

"Well?" Andrew was impatient.

"By trying to 'open your mind', as you put it, you'd just be surrendering your sane consciousness to a brooding insanity. The human mind is pretty complex, son. About nine-tenths of your brain is dark, shadowy, all animal instinct. Only the conscious fraction can evaluate—use logic. The balance between the two is pretty tricky at best. I wouldn't fool around with it, if I were you. Listen, Andy, I know you were born on Mars, I know how you feel. You feel at home here, don't you?"

"Yes, but that doesn't mean—"

"You resent men like Spade and Kater, coming here for the money that's in it, don't you?"

"Not really. Well, yes, but—"

There was a Mars-born kid with Kingslander, Andy. Remember the log? He was the first to go. In a place like this, imagination is worse than smallpox. You're the focal point where trouble would start, if it started. That's why I picked men like Spade and Kater—insensitive, unimaginative—for the first groundwork here. I've had my eye on you from the beginning, Andy, and you reacted just about the way I expected. I'm sorry, but you'll have to go."

Andrew clenched his fists in his pocket, speaking dry-mouthed. "But if I was right—wouldn't it be easier for them to contact someone like me? Won't you try to see it *my* way?" He made a final, hopeless appeal. "Won't you let me stay? I *know* I'm safe here—I know they won't hurt me, whatever happens to the others. Take my gun if you want to—keep me in handcuffs, even—but don't send me back!"

Reade's voice was flat and final. "If I had any doubts, I wouldn't have them after that. Every word you say is just making it worse. Leave while you still can, Andy."

Andrew gave up. "All right. I'll start back now, if you insist."

"I do." Reade turned away and hurried back toward the crew, and Andrew went into the tent and started packing rations in his blanket-roll for the march. The pack was clumsy, but not a tenth as heavy as the load he'd packed on the way up here. He jerked the straps angrily tight, hoisted the roll to his shoulder, and went out.

Reade was waiting for him. He had Andrew's pistol.

"You'll need this." He gave it to him; hauled out his notebook and stabbed a finger at the sketchy map he had drawn on their way over the mountains. "You've got your compass? Okay, look; this is the place where our route crossed the mailcar track from Mount Denver to the South Encampment. If you camp there for a few hours, you can hitch a ride on the mail-car—there's one every other day—into Mount Denver. When you get there, look up Montray. He's getting the expedition together back there." Reade tore the leaf from his notebook, scribbling the address on the back. Andrew lifted an eyebrow; he knew Reade had planned the expedition

in two sections, to prevent the possibility that they, trap would vanish without even a search-party sent after them.

"He won't have things ready, of course, but tell him to hurry it up, and give him all the help you can. Tell him what we're up against."

"You mean what you're up against. Are you sure you can trust me to run your errands in Mount Denver?"

"Don't be so grim about it," Reade said gently. "I know you want to stay, but I'm only doing my duty the way I see it. I have to think of everybody, not just you—or myself." He gripped Andrew's shoulder. "If things turn out all right, you can come back when they're all under control. Good luck, Andy."

"And if they don't?" Andrew asked, but Reade had turned away.

It had been a rough day. Andrew sat with his back against a boulder, watching the sun drop swiftly toward the reddish range of rock he had climbed that afternoon. Around him the night wind was beginning to build up, but he had found a sheltered spot between two boulders; and in his heated sleeping-bag, could spend a comfortable night even at sixty-below temperatures.

He thought ahead while he chewed the tasteless Mar-beef—Reade had outfitted the expedition with Space Service surplus—and swallowed hot coffee made from ice painstakingly scraped from the rocks. It had taken Reade, and five men, four days to cross the ridge. Travelling light, Andrew hoped to do it in three. The distance was less than thirty miles by air, but the only practicable trail wound in and out over ninety miles, mostly perpendicular. If a bad sandstorm built up, he might not make it at all, but anyone who spent more than one season on Mars took that kind of risk for granted.

The sun dropped, and all at once the sky was ablaze with stars. Andrew swallowed the last of his coffee, looking up to pick out the Heavenly Twins on the horizon—the topaz glimmer of Venus, the blue star-sapphire that was Earth. Andrew had lived on Earth for a few years in his teens, and hated it; the thick moist air, the dragging feel of too much gravity. The close-packed cities nauseated him with their smell of smoke and grease and human sweat. Mars air was thin and cold and scentless. His parents had hated Mars the same way he had hated Earth—they were biologists in the Xenozoology division, long since transferred to Venus. He had never felt quite at home anywhere, except for the few days he had spent at Xanadu. Now he was being kicked out of that too.

Suddenly, he swore. The hell with it, sitting here, feeling sorry for himself! He'd have a long day tomorrow, and a rough climb. As he unrolled his sleeping-bag, waiting for the blankets to warm, he wondered; how old *was* Xanadu?

Did it matter? Surely, if men could throw a bridge between the planets, they could build a bridge across the greater gap of time that separated them from these who had once lived on Mars. And if any man could do that, Andy admitted ungrudgingly, that man was John Reade. He pulled off his boots, anchored them carefully with his pack, weighted the whole thing down with rock, and crawled into the sack.

In the comforting warmth, relaxing, a new thought crossed his mind.

Whatever it was that had happened to him at Xanadu, he wasn't quite sure. The bump had confused him. But certainly *something* had happened. He did not seriously consider Reade's warning. He knew, as Reade could not be expected **to** know, that he had not suffered from a hallucination; had *not* been touched by the fringes of insanity. But he had certainly undergone a very strange experience. Whether it
had been subjective or objective, lie did not know; but he intended to find out.

How? He tried to remember a little desultory reading he had once done about telepathy. Although he had spoken glibly to Reade about 'opening his mind,' he really had not the faintest idea of what he had meant by the phrase. He grinned in the dark.

"Well, whoever and whatever you are," he said aloud, "*I'm* all ready and waiting. If you can figure out a way to communicate with me, come right ahead."

And the alien came.

"*I am Kamellin,*" it said.

I am Kamellin..

That was all Andrew could think. It was all his tortured brain could encompass. His head hurt, and the dragging sense of some actual, tangible force seemed to pull and twist at him. I AM KAMELLIN . . . KAMELLIN . . . KAMELLIN . . . it was like a tide that sucked at him, crowding out his own thoughts, dragging him under and drowning him. Andrew panicked; he fought it, thrashing in sudden frenzy, feeling arms and legs hit the sides of the sleeping-bag, the blankets twisted around him like an enemy's grappling hands.

Then the surge relaxed and he lay still, his breath loud in the darkness, and with fumbling fingers untangling the blankets. The sweat of fear was cold on his face, but the panic was gone.

For the force had not been hostile. It had only been— eager. Pathetically eager; eager as a friendly puppy is eager, as a friendly dog may jump up and knock a man down.

"Kamellin," Andrew said the alien word aloud, thinking that the name was not particularly outlandish. He hoped the words would focus his thoughts sufficiently for the alien to understand.

"Kamellin, come ahead, okay, but this time take it easy,

take it slow and easy. Understand?" Guardedly, he relaxed, hoping he would be able to take it if some unusual force were thrust at him; He could understand now why men had gone insane. If this—Kamellin—had hit him like that the *first* time-even now, when he understood and partly expected what was happening, it was an overwhelming flood, flowing through his mind like water running into a bottle. He lay helpless, sweating. The stars were gone, blanked out, and the howling wind was quiet—or was it that he no longer saw or heard? He hung alone in a universe of emptiness, and then, to his disembodied consciousness, came the beginning of— what? Not speech. Not even a mental picture. It was simply contact, and quite indescribable. And it said, approximately;

Greetings. At last. At last it has happened and we are both sane. I am Kamellin.

The wind was howling again, the stars a million flame-bright flares in the sky. Huddled in his blankets, Andrew felt the dark intruder in his brain ebb and flow with faint pressure as, their thoughts raced in swift question and answer. He whispered his own question aloud; otherwise Kamellin's thoughts flowed into his and intermingled with them until he found himself speaking Kamellin's thoughts.

"What are you? Was I right, then? Are you Martians discarnate intelligences?"

Not discarnate, we have always had bodies, or rather— we lived in bodies. But our minds and bodies were wholly separate. Nothing but our will tied them together. When one body died, we simply passed into another newborn body.

A spasm of claustrophobic terror grabbed at Andrew, and his flesh crawled. "You wanted—"

Kamellin's reassurance was immediate;

I do not want your body. You have, Kamellin fumbled for a concept to express what he meant, *you are a mature individual with a personality, a reasoning intelligence of your own. I would have to destroy that before your body could join with me in symbiosis.* His thoughts flared indignation; *That would not be honorable!*

"I hope all your people are as honorable as you are, then. What happened to the other expedition?"

He felt black anger, sorrow and desolation, breaking like tidal waves in his brain. *My people were maddened—I could not hold them back. They were not stable, what you would call, not sane. The time interval had been too long. There was much killing and death which I could not prevent.*

"If I could only find some way to tell Reade—"

It would be of no use. A time ago, I tried that. I attempted to make contact, easily, with a young mind that was particularly receptive to my thought. He did not go insane, and we, together, tried to tell Captain Kingslander what had happened to the others. But he believed it was more insanity, and when the young man was killed by one of the others, I had to dissipate again. I tried to reach Captain Kingslander himself, but the thought drove him insane—he was already near madness with his own fear.

Andrew shuddered. "God!" he whispered. "What can we do?"

I do not know. I will leave you, if you wish it. Our race is finally dying. In a few mare years we will be gone, and our planet will be safe for you.

"Kamellin, no!" Andrew's protest was immediate and genuine. "Maybe, together, we can think of some way to convince them."

The alien seemed hesitant now;

Would you be willing, then, to—share your body for a time? It will not be easy, it is never easy for two personalities to co-inhabit one body. I could not do it without your complete consent. Kamellin seemed to be thinking thoughts which were so alien that Andrew could grasp them only vaguely; only the concept of a meticulous honor remained to color his belief in Kamellin.

"What happened to your original host-race?"

He lay shivering beneath his heated blankets as the story unfolded in his mind. Kamellin's race, he gathered, had been humanoid—as that concept expressed itself, he sensed Kamellin's amusement; *Rather, your race is martianoid!* Yes, they had built the city the Earthmen called Xanadu, it was their one technological accomplishment which had been built to withstand time. *Built in the hope that one day we might return and reclaim it from the sand again,* Kamellin's soundless voice whispered, *The last refuge of our dying race.*

"What did you call the city?"

Kamellin tried to express the phonetic equivalent and a curious sound formed on Andrew's lips. He said it aloud, exploringly; "Shein-la Mahari." His tongue lingered on the liquid syllables. "What does it mean?"

The city of Mahari—Mahari, the little moon. Andrew found his eyes resting on the satellite Earthmen called Deimos. "Shein-la Mahari," he repeated. He would never call it Xanadu again.

Kamellin continued his story.

The host-race, Andrew gathered, had been long-lived and hardy, though by no means immortal. The minds and bodies—"minds," he impressed on Andrew, was not exactly the right concept—were actually two separate, wholly individual components. When a body died, the "mind" simply transferred, without any appreciable interval, into a newborn host; memory, although slightly impaired and blurred by such a transition, was largely retained. So that the consciousness of any one individual might extend, though dimly, over an almost incredible period of time.

The dual civilization had been a simple, highly mentalized one, systems of ethics and philosophy superseding one another in place of the rise and fall of governments. The physical life of the hosts was not highly technological. Xanadu had been almost their only such accomplishment, last desperate expedient of a dying race against the growing inhospitality of a planet gripped in recurrent, ever-worsening ice ages. They might have survived the ice alone, but a virus struck and decimated the hosts, eliminating most of the food animals as well. The birth-rate sank almost to nothing; many of the freed minds dissipated for lack of a host-body in which to incarnate.

Kamellin had a hard time explaining the next step. His kind could inhabit the body of anything which "had life, animal or plant. But they were subject to the physical limitations of the hosts. The only animals which 'survived disease and ice were the sand-mice and the moronic banshees; both so poorly organized, with nervous systems so faulty, that even when vitalized by the intelligence of Kamellin's race, they were incapable of any development. It was similar, Kamellin explained, to a genius who is imprisoned in the body of a helpless paralytic; his mind undamaged, but his body wholly unable to respond.

A few of Kamellin's people tried it anyhow, in desperation. But after a few generations of the animal hosts, they had degenerated terribly, and were in a state of complete nonsanity, unable even to leave the life-form to which they had bound themselves. For all Kamellin knew, some of his people still inhabited the banshees, making transition after transition by the faint, dim flicker of an instinct still alive, but hopelessly buried in generations of non-rational life.

The few sane survivors had decided, in the end, to enter the prickle-bushes; *spinosa mortis*. This was possible, although it, too, had drawbacks; the sacrifice of consciousness was the main factor in life as a plant. In the darkness of the Martian night, Andrew shuddered at Kamellin's whisper;

Immortality—without hope. An endless, dreamless sleep. We live, somnolent, in the darkness, and the wind, and wait—and forget. We had hoped that some day a new race might evolve on this world. But evolution here reached a dead end with the banshees and sand-mice. They are perfectly adapted to their environment and they have no struggle to survive: hence they need not evolve and change. When the Earthmen came, we had hope. Not that we might take their bodies. Only that we might seek help from them. But we were too eager, and my people drove out— killed—

The flow of thoughts ebbed away into silence.

Andrew spoke at last, gently.

"Stay with me for a while, at least. Maybe we can find a way."

It won't be easy, Kamellin warned.

"We'll try it, anyhow. How long ago—how long have you, well, been a plant?"

I do not know. Many, many generations—there is no consciousness of time. Many seasons. There is much blurring, Let me look at the stars with your eyes.

"Sure," Andrew consented.

The sudden blackness took him by surprise, sent a spasm of shock and terror through his mind; then sight came back and he found himself sitting upright, staring wide-eyed at the stars, and heard Kamellin's agonized thoughts;

It has been long—again the desperate, disturbing fumbling for some concept. *It has been nine hundred thousand of your years!*

Then silence; such abysmal grieved silence that Andrew was almost shamed before the naked grief of this man—he could not think of Kamellin except as a man—mourning for dead world. He lay down, quietly, not wanting to intrude on the sorrow of his curious companion.

Physical exhaustion suddenly overcame him, and he fell asleep.

"Was Mars like this in your day, Kamellin?" Andrew tossed the question cynically into the silence in his brain. Around him a freezing wind shifted and tossed at the crags, assailing the grip of his gauntleted hands on rock. He didn't expect any answer. The dark intruder had been dormant all day; Andrew, when he woke, had almost dismissed the whole thing as a bizarre fantasy, born of thin air and impending madness.

But now the strange presence, like a whisper in the dark, was with him again.

Our planet was never hospitable. But why have you never discovered the roadway through the mountains?

"Give us time," Andrew said cynically. "We've only been on Mars a minute or two by your standards. What roadway?" *We cut a roadway through the mountains when we built Shein-la Mahari.*

"What about erosion? Would it still be there?" Kamellin had trouble grasping the concept of erosion. Rain and snow were foreign to his immediate experience. Unless the roadway had been blocked by a sandstorm, it should be there, as in Kamellin's day.

Andrew pulled himself to a ledge. He couldn't climb with Kamellin using part of his mind; the inner voice was distracting. He edged himself backward on a flat slab of rock, unstrapping his pack. The remnant of his morning coffee was hot in his canteen; he drank it while Kamellin's thoughts flowed through his. Finally he asked, "Where's this roadway?" Andrew's head reeled in vertigo. He lay flat on the ledge, dizzily grasping rock, while Kamellin tried to demonstrate his sense of direction. The whirl slowly quieted, but all he could get from the brain-shaking experience was that Kamellin's race had oriented themselves by at least eleven major compass points in what felt like four dimensions to Andrew's experience, oriented on fixed stars—his original host-race could see the stars even by daylight.

"But I can't, and anyway, the stars have moved."

I have thought of that Kamellin answered. *But this part: of the mountains is familiar to me. We are not far from the place. I will lead you there.*

"Lead on, MacDufl[7]."

The concept is unfamiliar. Elucidate.

Andrew chuckled. "I mean, which way do we go from here?"

The vertigo began to overcome him once more.

"No, no—not that again!"

Then I will have to take over all your senses—

Andrew's mental recoil was as instinctive as survival. The terror of that moment last night, when Kamellin forced him into nothingness, was still too vivid. "No! I suppose you could take over forcibly, you did once, but not without half killing me! Because this time I'd fight—I'd fight you like hell!"

Kamellin's .rage was a palpable pain in his mind. *Have you no honor of your own, fool from a mad world? How could I lie to you when my mind is part of your own? Wander as you please, I do not suffer and I am not impatient. I thought that you were weary of these rocky paths, no more!*

Andrew felt bitterly ashamed. "Kamellin—I'm sorry."

Silence, a trace of alien anger remaining.

Andrew suddenly laughed aloud. Alien or human, there were correspondences; Kamellin was sulking. "For goodness sake," he said aloud, "if we're going to share one body, let's not quarrel. I'm sorry if I hurt your feelings; this is all new to me. But you don't have to sit in the corner and turn up your nose, either!"

The situation suddenly struck him as too ridiculous to take seriously; he laughed aloud, and like a slow, pleasant ripple, he felt Kamellin's slow amusement strike through his own.

Forgive me if I offended. I am accustomed to doing as I please in a body I inhabit. I am here at your sufferance, and I offer apologies.

Andrew laughed again, in a curious doubled amusement, somehow eager to make amends. "Okay, Kamellin, take over. You know where I want to go—if you can get us there faster, hop to it."

But for the rest of his life he remembered the next hour with terror. His only memory was of swaying darkness and dizziness, feeling his legs take steps he had not ordered, feeling his hands slide on rock and being unable to clutch and save himself, walking blind and deaf and a prisoner in his own skull; and ready to go mad with the horror of it. Curiously enough, the saving thought had been; Kamellin's able to stand it. He isn't going to hurt us.

When sight and sense and hearing came back, and full orientation with it, he found himself at the mouth of a long, low canyon which stretched away for about twelve miles, perfectly straight. It was narrow, less than fifteen feet wide. On either side, high dizzy cliffs were cut sharply away; he marvelled at the technology that had built this turnpike road.

The entrances were narrow, concealed between rock, and deeply drifted with sand; the hardest part had been descending, and later ascending, the steep, worn-away steps that led down into the floor of the canyon. He had struggled and cursed his way down the two-foot steps, wishing that the old Martians had had shorter legs; but once down, he had walked the whole length in less than two hours—travelling a distance, which Reade had covered in three weary days of rock-climbing.

And beside the steps was a ramp down which vehicles could be driven; had it been less covered with sand, Andrew could have slid down!

When he finally came to the end of the canyon road, the nearly-impassible double ridge of mountains lay behind him. From there it was a simple matter to strike due west and intersect the road from Mount Denver to the spaceport. There he camped overnight, awaiting the mailcar. He was awake with the first faint light, and lost no time in gulping a quick breakfast and strapping on his pack; for the mail-cars were rocket-driven (in the thin air of Mars, this was practical) and travelled at terrific velocities along the sandy barren flats; he'd have to be alert to flag it down.

He saw it long before it reached him, a tiny cloud of dust; he hauled off his jacket and, shivering in the freezing air, flagged furiously. The speck grew immensely, roared, braked to a stop; the driver thrust out a head that was only two goggled eyes over a heavy dustkerchief.

"Need a ride?"

Protocol on Mars demanded immediate identification.

"Andrew Slayton—I'm with the Geographic Society—Reade's outfit back in the mountains at Xanadu. Going back to Mount Denver for the rest of the expedition."

The driver gestured. "Climb on and hang on. I've heard about that gang. Reade's Folly, huh?"

"That's what they call it." He settled himself on the seatless floor—like all Martian vehicles, the rocket-car was a bare chassis without doors, seats or sidebars, stripped ,to lower freight costs—and gripped the rail. The driver looked down at him, curiously;

"I heard about that place Xanadu. Jinxed, they say. You must be the first man since old Torchevsky, to go there and get back safe. Reade's men all right?"

"They were fine when I left," Andrew said.

"Okay. Hang on," the driver warned, and at Andrew's nod, cut in the rockets and the sand-car leaped forward, eating up the desert.

Mount Denver was dirty and smelly after the clean coldness of the mountains. Andrew found his way through the maze of army barracks and waited in the officers' Rec quarters while a call-system located Colonel Reese Montray.

He hadn't been surprised to find out that the head of the other half of the expedition was a Colonel in active service; after all, within the limits imposed by regulations, the Army was genuinely anxious for Reade to find something at Xanadu. A genuine discovery might make some impression on the bureaucrats back on Earth; they might be able to revive public interest in Mars, get "some more money and supplies instead of seeing everything diverted to Venus and Europa.

Montray was a tall thin man with a heavy Lunar Colony accent, the tiny stars of the Space Service glimmering above the Army chevrons on his sleeve. He gestured Andrew into a private office and Listened, with a bored look, up to the point where he left Reade; then began to shoot questions at him.

"Has he proper chemical testing equipment for the business? Protection against gas—chemicals?"

"I don't think so," Andrew said. He'd forgotten Reade's theory about hallucinogens in *spinosa mortis;* so much had happened since that it didn't seem to make much difference.

"Maybe we'd better get it to him. I can wind things up here in an hour or so, if I have to, I've only got to tell the Commander what's going on. He'll put me on detached duty. You can attend to things here at the Geographic Society Headquarters, can't you, Slayton?"

Andrew said quietly, "I'm going back with you, Colonel Montray. And you won't need gas equipment. I did make contact with one of the old Martians."

Montray sighed and reached for the telephone. "You can tell Dr.

Cranston all about it, over at the hospital."

"I knew you'd think I was crazy," Andrew said in resignation, "but I can show you a pass that will take you through the Double Ridge in three hours, not three days—less, if you have a sand-car."

The Colonel's hand was actually on the telephone, but he didn't pick it up. He leaned back and looked at Andrew curiously. "You discovered this pass?"

"Well, yes and no, sir." He told his story quickly, skipping over the parts about Kamellin, concentrating on the fact of the roadway. Montray heard him out in silence, then picked up the telephone, but he didn't call the hospital. Instead he called an employment bureau in the poorer part of Mount Denver. While he waited for the connection he looked uncertainly at Andrew and muttered, "I'd have to go out there in a few weeks anyhow. They said, if Reade got well started, he could use Army equipment—" he broke off and spoke into the clicking phone.

"Montray here for the Geographic. I want twenty roughnecks for desert work. Have them here in two hours." He held down the contact button, dialed again, this time to call Dupont, Mars Limited, and requisition a first-class staff chemist, top priority. The third call, while Andrew waited—admiring, yet resenting the smoothness with which Montray could pull strings, was to the Martian Geographic Society headquarters; then he heaved himself up out of his chair and said, "So that's that. I'll buy your story, Slayton. You go down—" he scrawled on a pink form, "and commandeer an Army sand-bus that will hold twenty roughnecks and equipment. If you've told the truth, the Reade expedition is already a success and the Army will take over. And if you haven't—" he made a curt gesture of dismissal, and Andrew knew that if anything went wrong, he'd be better off in the psycho ward than anywhere Montray could get at him.

When Army wheels started to go round, they ran smoothly. Within five hours they were out of Mount Denver with an ease and speed which made Andrew—accustomed to the penny-pinching of Martian Geographic—gape in amazement. He wondered if this much string-pulling could have saved Kingslander. Crammed in the front seat of the sand-bus, between Montray and the Dupont chemist, Andrew reflected gloomily on the military mind and its effect on Reade. What would Reade say when he saw Andrew back again?

The wind was rising. A sandstorm on Mars makes the worst earthly wind look like a breeze to fly kites; the Army driver swore helplessly as he tried to see through the blinding sand, and the roughnecks huddled under a tarpaulin, coarse bandanas over their eyes, swearing in seven languages. The chemist braced his kit on his knees—he'd refused to trust it to the baggage-bins slung under the chassis next to the turbines—and pulled his dustkerchief over his eyes as the hurricane wind buffeted the sand-bus. Montray shouted above the roar, "Doesn't that road of yours come out somewhere along here?"

Shielding his eyes, Andrew peered over the low windbreak and crouched again, wiping sand from his face. "Half a mile more."

Montray tapped the driver on the shoulder. "Here."

The bus roared to a stop and the wind, unchallenged by the turbine noise, took over in their ears.

Montray gripped his wrist. "Crawl back under the canvas and we'll look at the map."

Heads low, they crawled in among the roughnecks; Montray flashed a pocket light on the "map", which was no more than a rough aerial photo taken by a low flier over the ridge. At one edge were a group of black dots which might or might not have been Xanadu, and the ridge itself was a confusing series of blobs; Andrew rubbed a gritty finger over the photo.

"Look, this is the route we followed; Reade's Pass, we named it. Kingslander went this way; a thousand feet lower, but too much loose rock. The canyon is about here—that dark line could be it."

"Funny the flier who took the picture didn't see it." Montray raised his voice. "All out—let's march!"

"In'a dees' weather?" protested a gloomy voice, touching off a chorus of protest. Montray was_ inflexible. "Reade might be in bad trouble. Packs, everybody."

Grumbling, the roughnecks tumbled out and adjusted packs and dust-bandanas. Montray waved the map-photo at Andrew; "Want this?"

"I can find my way without it."

A straggling disorderly line, they began, Andrew leading, He felt strong and confident. In his mind Kamellin lay dormant and that pleased him too; he needed every scrap of his mind to fight the screaming torment of the wind. It sifted its way through his bandana and ate into his skin, though he had greased his face heavily with lanolin before leaving the barracks. It worked, a gritty nuisance, through his jacket and his gloves. But it was his own kind of weather; Mars weather. It suited him, even though he swore as loud as anyone else.

Montray swore too, and spat grit from his throat.

"Where is this canyon of yours?"

A little break in the hillocky terrain led northward, then the trail angled sharply, turned into the lee of a bleak canyon wall. "Around there." Andrew fell back, letting Montray lead, while he gave a hand to the old man from DuPont.

Montray's angry grip jerked at his elbow; Andrew's bandana slid down and sailed away on the storm, and the chemist stumbled and fell to his knees. Andrew bent and helped the old fellow to his feet before he thrust his head around to Montray and demanded, "What the hell is the big idea?"

"That's what I'm asking you!" Montray's furious voice shouted the storm down. Andrew half fell around the turn, hauled by Montray's grip; then gulped, swallowing sand, while the wind bit unheeded at his naked cheeks. For there was now no trail through the ridge. Only a steep slope of rock lay before them, blank and bare, every crevice filled to the brim with deep-drifted sand.

Andrew turned to Montray, his jaw dropping. "I don't understand this at all, sir," he" gulped, and went toward the edge. There was no sign of ramp or steps.

"I do." Montray bit his words off and spat them at Andrew. "You're coming back to Mount Denver—under arrest!"

"Sir, I came through here yesterday! There was a wide track, a ramp, about eleven feet wide, and at one side there were steps, deep steps—" he moved toward the edge, seeking signs of the vanished trailway. Montray's grip on his arm did not loosen. "Yeah, and a big lake full of pink lemonade down at the bottom. Okay, back to the bus."

The roughnecks crowded behind 'them, close to the deep-deep-drifted sand near the spires of rock Andrew had sighted as landmarks on either side of the canyon. One of them stepped past Montray, glaring at the mountain of sand.

"All the way out here for a looney!" he said in disgust.

He took another step—then suddenly started sinking-stumbled, flailed and went up to his waist in the loose-piled dust.

"Careful—get back—" Andrew yelled. "You'll go in over your heads!" The words came without volition.

The man in the sand stopped in mid-yell, and his kicking arms stopped throwing up dust. He looked thoughtfully up at the other roughnecks. "Colonel", he said slowly, "I don't think Slayton's so crazy. I'm standing on a step, and there's another one under my knee. Here, dig me out." He began to brush sand away with his two hands. "Big steps—"

Andrew let out a yell of exultation, bending to haul the man free. "That's IT," he shouted. "The sandstorm last night just blew a big drift into the mouth of the canyon, that's all! If we could get through this drift, the rest lies between rock walls and around the next angle, the sand can't blow!"

Montray pulled binoculars from his pocket and focused them carefully. "In farther, I do see a break in the slope that looks like a canyon," he said. "If you look at it quick, it seems to be just a flat patch; but with the glasses, you can see that it goes down between walls . . . but there's a hundred feet of sand, at least, drifted into the entrance, and it might as well be a hundred miles. We can't wade through that." He frowned, looking around at the sandbus. "How wide did you say this canyon was?"

"About fifteen feet. The ramp's about eleven feet wide."

Montray's brow ridged. "These busses are supposed to cross drifts up to eighty feet We'll chance it. Though if I take an army sandbus in there, and get it stuck in a drift, we might as well pack for space."

Andrew felt grim as they piled back into the bus. Montray displaced the driver and took the controls himself. He gave the mail} rocket high power; the bus shot forward, its quickly-extruded glider units sliding lightly, without traction, over the drifted sand. It skidded a little as Montray gunned it for the turn;, the chassis hit the drift like a ton of lead. Swearing prayerfully, Montray slammed on the auxiliary rockets, and it roared—whined—sprayed up sand like a miniature sirocco, then, mercifully, the traction lessened, the gliders began to function, and the sandbus skied lightly across the drift and down the surface of the monster ramp, into the canyon.

It seemed hours, but actually it was less than four minutes before the glider units scraped rock and Montray shut off the power and called two men to help him wind up the retractors . . . The gliders could be shot out at a moment's notice, because on Mars when they were needed, they were needed *fast,* but retracting them again was a long, slow business. He craned his neck over the windbreak, looking up at the towering walls, leaning at a dizzy angle over them. He whistled sharply. "This is no natural formation!"

"I told you it wasn't," Andrew said.

The man from Dupont scowled. "Almost anything can be a natural formation, in rock," he contradicted. "You say you discovered this pass, Slayton?"

Andrew caught Montray's eye and said meekly, "Yes, sir."

The sandbus cruised easily along the canyon floor, and up the great ramp at the other end; Montray drove stubbornly, his chin thrust out. Once he said, "Well, at least the Double Ridge—isn't a barricade any more," and once he muttered, "You could have discovered this by accident—delirious—and then rationalized it. . . ."

The Martian night was hanging, ready to fall, when the squat towers of the city reared up, fat and brown, against the horizon. From that distance they could see nothing of Reade's camp except a thin trail of smoke, clear against the purplish twilight. Vague unease stirred Andrew's mind and for the first time in hours, Kamellin's thoughts flickered dimly alive in the corridors of his brain.

I *am fearful. There is trouble.*

Montray shouted, and Andrew jerked up his head in dismay, then leaped headlong from the still-moving sandbus. He ran across the sand. Reade's tent lay in a smoking ruin on the red sand. His throat tight with dread, Andrew knelt and gently turned up the heavy form that lay, unmoving, beside the charred ruin.

Fat Kater had lost more than his shirt.

Montray finally stood up and beckoned three of the roughnecks. "Better bury him here," he said heavily, "and see if there's anything left unburned."

One of the men had turned aside and was noisily getting rid of everything he'd eaten for a week. Andrew felt like doing the same, but Montray's hand was heavy on his shoulder.

"Easy," he said. "No, I don't suspect you. He hasn't been dead more than an hour. Reade sent you away before it started, evidently." He gave commands; "No one else seems to have died in the fire. Spread out, two arid two, and look for Reade's men." He glanced at the sun, hovering too close to the horizon; half an hour of sunlight, and Phobos would give light for another couple of hours—he said grimly, "After that, we get back to the bus and get out of here, fast. We can come back tomorrow, but we're not going to wander around here by Deimos-light." He unholstered his pistol.

Don't, said the eerie mentor in Andrew's brain, *no weapons.*

Andrew said urgently, "Colonel, have the roughnecks turn in their pistols! Kingslander's men killed each other pretty much like this!"

"And suppose someone meets a banshee? And Reade's men all have pistols, and if they're wandering around, raving mad—"

The next hour was nightmarish, dark phantoms moving shoulder to shoulder across the rock-needled ground; muttered words, far away the distant screams of a banshee somewhere. Once the crack of a pistol cut the night; it developed—after the roughnecks had all come running in, and half a dozen random shots had been fired, fortunately wounding no one—that one man had mistaken a rock-spire for a banshee. Montray cursed the man and sent him back to the sandbus with blistered ears. The sun dropped out of sight. Phobos, a vast purple balloon, sketched the towers of the city in faint shadows on the sand. The wind wailed and flung sand at the crags.

An abrupt shout of masculine hysteria cut the darkness; Montray jumped, stumbled and swore. "If this is another false alarm—"

It wasn't. Somebody flashed an electric torch on the sand; Mike Fairbanks, a bullet hole cleanly through his temple, lay on the sand that was only a little redder than his blood.

That left Hansen, Webber—and John Reade.

I can find them: let me find them! Before something worse happens—

"Sir, I think I can find the others. I told you about Kamellin. This proves—"

"Proves nothing," grunted Montray. "But go ahead." Andrew felt coldly certain that inside the pocket of his leathers, Montray's finger was crooked around a trigger trained on his heart. Tense and terrified, Andrew let Kamellin lead him. How did he know that this was not an elaborate trap for the Earthmen? For Kamellin led them straight beneath the walls of the city and to an open door—an open door, and three expeditions had blasted without success!

One of my people has taken over one of your men. He must have found the hidden door. If only he is still sane, we have a bare chance. ...

"Stop there," Montray ordered curtly.

"Stop there," echoed a harsh wild voice, and the disheveled figure of John Reade, hatless, his jacket charred, appeared in the doorway. "Andrew!" His distorted shout broke into a sobbing gasp of relief, and he pitched headlong into Andrew's arms. "Andy, thank God you're here! They—shot me—"

Andrew eased him gently to the ground. Montray bent over the old man, urging, "Tell us what happened, John." "Shot in the side—Andy you were right—something got

Spade first, then Kater fired the tent—Spade rushed him, shot Mike Fairbanks—then—then, Andy, it got me, it sneaked inside me, inside my head when I wasn't looking, inside my head—"

His" head lolled on Andrew's shoulder.

Montray let go his wrist with a futile gesture. "He's hurt pretty bad. Delirious."

"His head's as clear as mine. He's fainted, that's all," Andrew protested. "If we bring him around, he can tell us—"

"He'll be in no shape to answer questions," said the scientist from Dupont, very definitely, "not for a long time. Montray, round up the men; we've got to get out of here in a hurry—"

"Look out!" shouted somebody. A pistol shot crashed and the scream of an injured man raised wild echoes. Andrew felt his heart suck and turn over; then he suddenly sank into blindness and felt himself leap to his feet and run toward the voices. Kamellin had taken over!

Spade Hansen, tottering on his feet, stumbled toward them. His shirt hung raggedly in charred fragments. Through some alien set of senses, like seeing double, Andrew sensed the presence of another, one of Kamellin's kind.

If I can get through to him—"

Montray cocked, levelled his pistol.

"Hansen!" His voice cracked a whip, "stand where you are!"

Spade yelled something.

"Po'ki hai marrai nic Mahari—"

"You fool! They are afraid of us! Stand back!

Spade flung himself forward and threw his pistol to the ground at Andrew's feet. *"Kamellin!"* .he screamed, but the voice was not his own. Andrew's heart thudded. He stepped forward, letting the dark intruder in his mind take over all his senses again. A prisoner, he heard the alien voice shouting, felt his throat spewing forth alien syllables. There were

shouts, a despairing howl, then somewhere two pistols cracked together and Andrew flickered back to full consciousness to see Hansen reel, stumble and fall inert. Andrew sagged, swayed; Montray held him upright, and Andrew whispered incredulously, "You shot him!"

"I didn't," Montray insisted. "Rick Webber burst out of that doorway—fired into the crowd. Then—"

"Is Rick dead too?"

"As a doornail." Montray gently lowered the younger man to the sand beside Reade. "You were raving yourself, for a minute, young Slayton." He shouted angrily at the roughneck who had shot, "You didn't have to kill Webber! A bullet in the leg would have stopped him!"

"He ran right on me with the gun—"

Montray sighed and struck his forehead with his clenched hands. "Somebody made a stretcher for Reade and one for the kid here."

"I'm all right." Andrew shoved Montray's hand aside; bent to look at Reade.

"He's in a bad way," the man from Dupont said "We'd better get them both back to Mount Denver while there's time." He looked sharply at Andrew. "You had better take it easy, too. You went shouting mad yourself, for a minute." He stood up, turning to Montray.

"I think my theory is correct. Virus strains can live almost indefinitely where the air is dry. If such a plague killed off the people who built the city, it would explain why everyone who's come up here has caught it—homicidal and suicidal."

"That isn't it—"

Montray checked him forcibly. "Slayton, you're a sick man too. You'll have to trust our judgment," he said. He tucked his own coat around Reade and stood up, his face gray in the fading moonlight. "I'm going to the governor," he said, "and have this place put off limits. Forty-two men dead of an unknown Martian virus, that's too much. Until we get the money and the men to launch a full-scale medical project and knock it out, there won't be any more private expeditions—or public ones, either. The hell with Xanadu." He cocked his pistol and fired the four-shot signal to summon any stragglers.

Two of the men improvised a stretcher and began to carry Reade's inert

Body toward the sandbus. Andrew walked close, steadying the old man's limp form with his hands. He was beginning to doubt himself. Under the setting moon, the sand biting his face, he began to ask himself if Montray had been right. Had he dreamed, then rationalized? Had he dreamed Kamellin? *Kamellin?* he asked.

There was no answer from the darkness in his mind. Andrew smiled grimly, his arm easing Reade's head in the rude litter. If Kamellin had ever been there, he was gone, and there was no way to prove any of it—and it didn't matter any more.

"... therefore, with regret, I am forced to move that project Xanadu be shelved indefinitely," Reade concluded. His face was grim and resigned, still thin from his long illness. "The Army's attitude is inflexible, and lacking men, medics and money, it seems that the only thing to do with Xanadu is to stay away from it."

"It goes without saying," said the man at the head of the table, "that we all appreciate what Major Reade and Mr. Slayton have been through. Gentlemen, no one likes to quit. But in the face of this, I have no alternative but to second Major Reade's suggestion. Gentlemen, I move that the Martian chapter of the Geographic Society be closed out, and all equipment and personnel transferred to Aphrodite Base Twelve, South Venus."

The vote was carried without dissent, and Reade and Andrew, escaping the bombardment of questions, drifted into the cold sunlight of the streets. They walked for a long time without speaking. Reade said at last:

"Andy, we did everything we could. Montray put his own commission in jeopardy for us. But this project has cost millions already. We've just hit the bottom of the barrel, that's all."

Andrew hunched his shoulders. "I could be there in three days."

"I'd like to try it, too." Reade sounded grim. " But forget it, Andy. Shein-la Mahara is madness and death. Forget it. Go home—"

"Home? Home where? To Earth?" Andrew broke off, staring. *What* had Reade said?

"Say that again. The name of the city.*"

"Shein-la Mahari, the city of—" Reade gulped. "What in the *hell*—" he looked at Andy in despair. "I thought I could forget, convince myself it never happened. It left me when Hansen shot me. We've *got* to forget it, Andy—at least until we're on the ship going home."

"Ship, hell! We're not going back to Earth, Reade!"

"Here, here," said Reade, irritably, '"Who's not going?"

Andrew subsided, thinking deeply. Then, with a flash of inspiration, he turned to Reade. "John, who owns the Society's test animals?"

Reade rubbed his forehead. "Nobody, I guess. They sure won't bother shipping a few dogs and chimps out to Venus! I've got authority to release them—I guess I'll turn them over to Medic. Why? You want a dog? A monkey? What for?" He stopped in his tracks, glaring. "What bug have you got in your brain now?"

"Never mind. You're going back to Earth by the next ship."

"Don't be in such a rush," Reade grumbled, "The *Erden-luft* won't blast for a week."

Andrew grinned. "John, those animals are pretty highly organized. I wonder—"

Reade's eyes met his in sudden comprehension. "Good lord, I never thought of that! Come on, let's hurry!"

At the deserted shack where the Society's animals were kept, a solitary keeper glanced indifferently at Reade's credentials and let them in. Reade and Andrew passed the dogs without comment, glanced at and rejected the one surviving goat, and passed on to the caged chimpanzees.

"Well, either I'm crazy or this is it," he said, and listened for that inner answer, the secret intruder in his brain. And after a long time, dimly, it came as if Kamellin could not at once reestablish lapsed contact.

I should have left you. There is no hope now, and I would rather die with my people than survive as a prisoner in your mind.

"No!" Andrew swung to face the chimpanzee. "Could you enter that living creature without his consent?"

There was a tightness across his diaphragm, as if it were his own fate, not Kamellin's, that was being decided.

That creature could not give consent.

"I'm sorry, I tried—"

Kamellin's excitement almost burst into speech. *No, no, he is perfectly suited, for he is highly organized, but lacking intelligence—*

"A chimp's intelligent—"

A shade of impatience, as if Kamellin were explaining to a dull child; *A brain, yes, but he lacks something—will, spirit, soul, volition—*

"A chimp can be taught to do almost anything a man can—"

Except talk, communicate, use real reason. Yo« cannot entirely grasp this either, I know. It was the first time Andrew had been allowed to glimpse the notion that Kamellin did not consider Andrew his complete equal. *The banshees are the first stage: A physical brain, consciousness, but no intelligence. They cannot be organized. Then your creature, your primate mammal, intelligence but no soul. However, when vitalized by true reason. . . .* Kamellin's thought-stream cut off abruptly, but not before Andrew had caught the concept, *What does the Earthman think he is, anyhow?*

Kamellin's thoughts were troubled; *Forgive me, I had no right to give you that. . .*

"Inferiority complex?" Andrew laughed.

You do not function on the level of your soul. 'You're aware almost exclusively in your five senses and your reasoning intelligence. But your immortal mind is somehow stunted: You humans have slid into a differed time-track somehow, and you live only in three dimensions, losing memory—

"I don't believe in the soul, Kamellin."

That is the point I am trying to make, Andrew.

Reade touched his shoulder. "You give me the creeps, talking to yourself. What now?"

They picked out a large male chimp and sat looking at it while it grimaced at them with idiotic mildness. Andrew felt faint distaste. "Kamellin in that thing?"

Reade chuckled. "Quit being anthropomorphic. *That thing* is a heck of a lot better adapted to We on Mars than you are—look at the size of the chest—and Kamellin will know it, if you don't!" He paused. "After the switch, how can we communicate with Kamellin?"

Andrew relayed the question, puzzled. Finally he said, "I'm not sure. We're using straight thoughts and he can't get any notion of the *-form* of our language, any more than I can of his. Reade, can a chimp learn to talk?"

"No chimp ever has."

"I mean, if a chimp *did* have the intelligence, the reasoning power, the drive to communicate in symbols or language, would its vocal cords and the shape of his mouth permit it!"

"I wouldn't bet on it," Reade said, "I'm no expert on monkey anatomy, though. I wouldn't bet against it either. Why? Going to teach Kamellin English?"

"Once he leaves me, there won't be any way to communicate except the roughest sort of sign language!"

"Andy, we've got to figure out some way! We can't let that knowledge be lost to us! Here we have a chance at direct contact with a mind that was alive when the city was built—"

"That's not the important part," Andrew said. "Ready, Kamellin?"

Yes. And I thank you eternally. Your world and mine lie apart, but we have been brothers. I salute you, my friend. The voice went still. The room reeled, went into a sick bluer—

"Are you all right?" Reade peered anxiously down at Andrew. Past him, they both realized that the big chimpanzee—no, Kamellin!—was looking over Reade's shoulder. Not the idiot stare of the monkey. Not human, either. Even the posture of the animal was different.

Andrew—recognized—Kamellin.

And the—difference—in his mind, was gone.

Reade was staring; "Andy, when you fell, he jumped forward and *caught* you! No monkey would do that!"

Kamellin made an expressive movement of his hands.

Andrew said, "A chimp's motor reflexes are marvelous, with a human—no, a *better* than human intelligence, there's practically no limit to what he can do." He said, tentatively, "Kamellin?"

"Will the chimp recognize that?"

"Look, Reade—will you remember something, as a favor to me? He—the chimp—is *not* a freak monkey! He is Kamellin—my close personal friend—and a damned sight more intelligent than either of us!"

Reade dropped his eyes. "I'll try."

"Kamellin?"

And Kamellin spoke. Tentatively, hoarsely, mouthily, as if with unfamiliar vocal equipment, he spoke. "An—drew," he said slowly. "Shein. La. Mahari." They had each reached the extent of their vocabulary in the other's language. Kamellin walked to the other cages, with the chimpanzee's rolling scamper which somehow had, at the same time, a controlled and fluid dignity that was absolutely new. Reade dropped on a bench. "I'll be damned," he said. "But do you realize what you've done, Andrew? A talking monkey. At best, they'd call us a fraud. At. worst the scientists would end up dissecting him. We'll never be able to prove anything or tell anyone!"

"I saw that all along," Andrew said bitterly, and dropped to the bench. Kamellin came and squatted beside them, alert, with an easy stillness.

Suddenly Andrew looked up. "There are about twenty chimps. Not enough. But there's a good balance, male to female, and they can keep up a good birth rate—"

"What in the—"

"Look," Andrew said excitedly, "it's more important to preserve the Martian race—the last few sane ones—than to try convincing the Society—; we probably couldn't anyhow. We'll take the chimps to Shein-la Mahari. Earthmen never go there, so they won't be molested for a while, anyhow— probably not for a hundred years or so! By that time, they'll have been able to—to reclaim their race a little, gain back their culture, and there'll be a colony of intelligent beings, monkeylike in form but not monkeyish. We can leave records of this. In a hundred years or so—"

Reade looked at him hesitantly, his imagination gripped, against his will, by Andrew's vision. "Could they survive?"

"Kamellin told me that the city was—time-sealed, he called it, and in perfect order." He looked down at the listening stillness of Kamellin and was convinced that the

Martian understood; certainly Kamellin's reception of telepathy must be excellent, even if Andrew's was not.

"It was left that way—waiting for a race they could use, if one evolved. Chimps have terrific dexterity, once they're guided by intelligence. They made their food chemically, by solar power, and there are heat units, records—just waiting."

Reade stood up and started counting the chimpanzees. "We'll probably lose our jobs and our shirts—but well try it, Andy. Go borrow a sandbus—I've still got good contacts." He scribbled a note on a scrap of paper he found in his pocket, then added grimly, "But don't forget; we've still got to be on the *Erdenluft* when it lifts off."

"We'll be on it."

Once again Andrew Slayton stood on the needled desert for a last look at the squat towers of Shein-la Mahari. He knew he would never come back.

Reade, his white shock of hair bent, stood beside him. Around them the crowd of Martians stood motionless, with a staid dignity greater than human, quietly waiting.

"No," Reade said half to himself, "it wouldn't work, Andy. Kamellin might take a chance on you, but you'd both regret it."

Andrew did not move or answer, still looking hungrily up at the glareless ramparts. If I could only write a book about it, he was thinking. The day they had spent had been what every inter-planetary archaeologist dreams about in his most fantastic conjectures. The newly-incarnate Martians had been gratefully receptive to Reade's expressive sign-language and the tour of the city was a thing past all their wildest imagination.

Beneath the sand of centuries Shein-la Mahari was more than a city; it was a world. Never would they forget the heart-stopping thrill when a re-inhabited Martian, working with skill and inhuman awareness, had uncovered the ancient machinery of the water supply, connected to the miles-deep underground lakes, and turned great jets of water into hydroponic gardens; seeds long in storage had instantly bubbled into Sprouting life. A careful engineer, her monkeylike paws working with incredible skill, had set sealed power units to humming. Rations, carefully time-sealed against emergency, were still edible. Reade and Andrew had shared the strangest meal of their lives with twenty-odd Martians—and it was not the suddenly-controlled chimpanzees whose table manners had seemed odd. Martian conventions were a cultural pattern of unbelievable stability.

Nor would he ever forget the great library of glyphs inscribed on flexible sheets of Vanadium, the power-room of throbbing machinery—

"Forget it," Reade said roughly, "they'll probably send us to Titan—and who knows what we'll find there?"

"Yeah. We've got a spaceship to catch." Andrew climbed into the sandcar, leaning out to grasp Kamellin's paw—sensing that the Martian would understand the gesture, if not the words. "Goodbye, Kamellin. Good luck to all of you." He cut the rockets in and shot away in a thunderstorm of sand. He drove fast and dangerously. He would never see Shein-la Mahari again. He would leave Mars, probably forever. And forever he would be alone. ...

"They'll make out," said Reade gruffly, and put an arm around his shoulders. To his intense horror, Andrew discovered that he was blinking back scalding tears.

"Sure," he made himself say. "In a few hundred years they'll be way ahead of Earth. Look what seventy-odd pilgrims did in North America, on our own planet! Synthetics-power—maybe even interstellar travel. They'd visited Earth once, before the plagues that killed them, Kamellin told me." The sandcar roared around the rock-wall and Shein-la Mahari was gone. Behind them Andrew heard a rumble and a dull, groundshaking thunder. The pass behind them crashed in ruin; the Ridge was impassable again. Kamellin and his Martians would have their chance, unmolested by Earthmen, for at least a few years—

"I wonder," Reade mused, "which race will discover the other first... ?